CW00968944

Table of Cc

Club Sin
Room Twenty-Five

A Multiple Pleasure Reverse Harem Romance

Autumn Seave

This book is a work of fiction. Any resemblance to persons, living or dead, or places, events or locations is purely coincidental.

Upon entering Club Sin, you are consenting to the following:

1. You are STI/STD free.

2. You are healthy and able to engage in or observe sexual activity at Club Sin.

3. You are on or have brought birth control of your choice.

4. You consent to engage in the kink of your choice upon entering the room of your choice. Anyone is welcome in the room that represents their kink with consent; privacy is maintained when requested. Multiple partners are common and encouraged at Club Sin.

5. No kink shaming allowed. People are free to explore and enjoy all their desires in a safe and consensual environment at Club Sin.

6. Honesty and communication are key to a satisfying experience at Club Sin.

7. Discretion and privacy are valued at Club Sin.

8. No cell phones are allowed in Club Sin.

9. Universal safe word at Club Sin is RED, unless otherwise agreed upon. Be aware of non-verbal cues.

At Club Sin we want you to have a satisfying experience. Go and play!

From the author of this book:

Regarding rule #1: Please be aware that in real life, sex clubs are not able to screen people for STI/STDs and many people may not disclose them. Some people do not even know they have an STI/STD and some STI/STDs are not screened for when individuals are tested (for example HSV1/HSV2) at the doctor's office. Someone may carry the disease and have no symptoms or outbreaks for years. For that reason, it is highly suggested that you always use condoms at a sex club for your protection and for the protection of anyone else you have sex with.

I feel that it is important not to shame people who have diseases like HSV1/HSV2 because doing so makes it harder for them to talk about it with their partners. Those who live with diseases like this should be able to continue to lead full sex lives with informed partners (this is my opinion and not necessarily the opinion of the other authors in this series).

Regarding Polyamory and Swinging in general: There are many different ways to "do" polyamory and Neve and Kieran are just one example. Hunter and Giles "do" the swinging lifestyle in their own way, too. The key to both is clear consent and communication.

Autumn Seave

Chapter One: Kieran

"THANKS, I HAD A GREAT time, too," Neve said as she hugged Jenna, a friend we'd known for several years.

"What did you think of Carter?" Jenna asked.

Neve smiled. "He was nice. Are you guys dating?"

Carter was new to our group and new to polyamory. He was good looking and friendly. I knew that Neve was hesitant about getting involved with someone new after her last partner, Ben, decided that he wanted to try to be monogamous with his other partner. We knew that it was a risk of our lifestyle but it still hurt her. She cared a lot for him.

I didn't have any real problem with Carter but I was worried about her being hurt again, too.

"No, we aren't," Jenna replied. "I thought he might be a good match for you."

Neve took my hand and leaned back into me. "I don't know if I'm ready yet, Jenna."

Jenna nodded. "I understand. Take your time. It was great seeing you again, Kieran."

"We'll see you at the next get-together," I replied with a smile.

Jenna turned towards her vehicle and I opened the door for Neve. "Are you ok?" I asked her as I climbed into the driver's side.

"Yes?" It was more of a question than a response. "I think so. You know, it's just been hard since Ben and I broke up. I mean, I'm still polyam but I just don't know if I have it in me to start dating again."

As I pulled out of the parking lot, I said, "I know what you mean. When Brad and Stephen moved to Germany, I thought I'd never want to date again, either. It's a little different because I still talk to Brad and I know at some point I'll see him again. It's hard, though."

"I hope you know I'm perfectly ok with your dating. I'm glad you've been meeting new people," she said.

"I appreciate that. It's just so hard to meet people that jive with us and who we are and how we try to live our lives. Remember that guy I went on a date with? Bryant? He was so nice. We had a couple of good dates and even made out a little bit. Then he tells me he's married and it's a 'don't ask, don't tell' type of deal. I'm polyamorous for Pete's sake. Why didn't he just tell me at the start? I just couldn't help but feel that since he didn't tell me right away his 'don't ask, don't tell' policy is more of a cheating type of deal. I couldn't be sure."

She nodded. "I totally agree with you. I would have been worried for you if you'd chosen to continue dating him."

Neve and I were polyamorous when we met. Before I even proposed, we talked through everything. We had some moments where we had to figure things out but it was just par for the course. By the time I proposed, we already knew that we wanted to keep hierarchy out of our relationship as much as possible. We didn't want any other partners to feel like they were secondary.

At one point, we were both dating the same guy, and he and Neve had a disagreement and broke up. It wasn't a major fight or anything. She just decided that she didn't want to continue having sex with him or continue their relationship. I felt like I should break up with him, too but she insisted that I should keep seeing him. He and I were still good. She didn't want me to end things just because the two of them weren't going to see each other for a while.

I kept seeing him for about six months. His jealousy became a problem, though. While I was able to keep our relationship separate from my relationship with Neve, he got upset every time I was with her, instead of him. Finally, I asked him what he wanted. He said he wanted me to leave Neve for him. When I said I wouldn't, he gave me the ultimatum. Him or her. I wouldn't choose so he left.

I guess he just wasn't ready to manage his feelings.

"You know what I miss?" Neve asked.

"What's that?"

"Threesomes. I miss being cuddled between you and someone else. I miss all the fun. But, I guess that's out the door. I can't seem to find anyone that I want to date right now and you haven't found anyone that has lasted more than a few dates. Plus, half the men you date are gay and not really into me," she said.

I laughed. This was true. I was bisexual and Neve was straight. But for some reason, the men I met were often gay. There had only been two bisexual men in our lives. One was the guy that got jealous. The other was my most recent partner, Brad. Brad wasn't dating Neve but he sure enjoyed being invited into our bedroom on occasion.

"Well, you know there are other options," I said.

"What do you mean?" she asked.

"Well, we're poly but that doesn't mean that we can't cross some lines here and there. We could maybe try swinging. Have you heard about that new club?"

"I've never really considered that," Neve said. "It just seems so..."

"Shady? It's not. Brad said he and Stephan have started to do some swinging. Just for fun. There are no expectations. People tend to be fairly open about what they're looking for. A lot of the time it's just a one-time thing but sometimes they become friends with a couple or even another guy and just play for fun. Personally, I kind of miss watching you get pleasured by another man. Even more fun when we make you scream together."

She laughed. "OK, so what's this new club?"

"Well, it's not really new. It's in the city. It's called Club Sin. I just recently heard about it so it's new to me. To us. Brad has friends here that he got to send me an invite so we could go. If you wanted," I said.

She was thinking. "What would it be like? Are people all running around naked? Would I have to have sex with anyone I didn't want to?"

I thought about what Brad told me. "No. You don't even have to have sex. There's a bar and a dance floor and clothing is required. Then there are rooms based on what you want to experience. Watching and being watched. Group sex. Spankings. Harder BDSM. Pretty much everything. And you can always say no thanks."

She didn't say anything but she was looking a little squirmy. Was she uncomfortable with the idea?

"It's just a suggestion, Neve. You know I'd never try to talk you into doing something you didn't want to do."

"I know," she said. "It's not that. I'm just a little turned on by the idea. Do you think a threesome would be as good with someone we didn't know very well as it would be with someone one or both of us was dating?"

"Maybe not the same. But it could still be good. I'd be there. I wouldn't let any harm come to you, you know. Plus, Brad said people who go to clubs like that are very well-behaved. It's all about consent, respect, and having fun within those expectations."

As we pulled into the driveway, Neve gave me a look.

"What?" I asked.

I got out of the car and we stood on either side by our doors for a moment.

Then she got this look in her eye and I knew what was on her mind.

"Race you to the bedroom!" she laughed. "Last one naked has to go down first."

I may have been stronger than Neve but she was small framed and she was a runner in college. She was through the door and down the hall before I even had my shoes off. By the time I got to the bedroom and was trying to get out of my jeans without falling over, Neve was laying naked on the bed.

"Okay, babe. You beat me fair and square. Let's see what we can do about relieving some of that frustration."

I moved to the end of the bed and she let her legs fall open. I loved how unselfconscious she was about exposing herself to me. It made it so much easier to enjoy her.

"Tell me," Neve said as I ran my finger up the length of her folds.

"Tell you what?" I asked.

"What would it be like? If we went to that club you were talking about?"

I continued to move my finger up and down, enjoying how wet she was. "Well, we'd probably have a drink. Just watch for a bit. See if there was anyone we were attracted to."

She sighed. "And if there was?"

I leaned forward and gave her a long, slow lick. Then I said, "I guess we'd try to get his attention. Which shouldn't be hard because I'm pretty sure all eyes would be on you the second we walked in."

"And once we got his attention?"

I took a minute to think of my answer while I swirled my tongue around her clit. She moaned lightly as I answered her. "We'd invite him to come sit with us. We'd flirt. I'm sure he'd be eager to move things forward but I know you'd make him wait for a little, sizing him up to get a feel for whether or not he was what you were looking for. It would be a bonus if he was bi, but honestly, I'd be happy to just watch you get fucked by someone that loved fucking as much as you do."

I went back to her wetness and tasted her, using the flat of my tongue to make as much contact as possible. When she began to quiver, I pulled back and said, "Eventually, he'd ask us to join him in a room. We'd agree. Inside the room, he'd get naked and then take off all your clothes. And between the two of us, we'd make you come in every way possible."

"Jesus, Kieran, that's enough. Make me come already!"

She pulled my head down between her legs and directed my mouth to where she wanted it. Her fingers wrapped in my hair and she pushed herself up towards me. I barely had to do a thing. I just let her grind against my mouth until she was quivering in uncontrollable spasms.

Chapter Two: Hunter

"What time will you be back tomorrow?" I asked Giles.

"Fairly early in the evening," he replied. "I wish I didn't have to go, though. I'd much rather be going to the club with you tonight."

I was planning to go to Club Sin. I might just stay for a few drinks. But who knew - maybe I would meet someone I liked and have some fun.

"I know," I said. "But this meeting is important. You might get all the funding you need for this project. And if you get the funding, you can start moving forward with it. You've been wanting to do this for a long time. You've put so much planning and work into it already."

Giles was crazy smart. That was one of the things I loved about him. I mean, I was smart, too. But when it came to tech, Giles was kind of a genius. He saw things differently than I did. It was like he thought in code or something. And he had the kind of creativity that didn't always come with tech knowledge. He worked for an app development company but he wanted to work for himself and if he got funding for this app idea of his that he'd been tweaking for the past year, he'd be able to branch out on his own.

"I know."

"Maybe you'll meet someone to have fun with while you're there," I suggested.

"Possibly. But I think I'm more likely to spend the whole night talking about apps and other techy stuff with this guy. And if he funds everything, I'll give him all the time he wants. Hell, I'd even blow him," Giles laughed.

"Please. Like that would be such a hardship for you."

Giles' phone buzzed and he looked at it. "My Uber is here. I'll call you when I get in, okay?"

"Okay," I said, giving him a gentle kiss. "Relax. You're going to be great."

After Giles left, I headed for the shower. I wasn't upset at the idea that Giles might give someone a blow job. We enjoyed swinging, together or on our own. When we first got together, we tried to be the happily married, monogamous gay couple that all of our friends seemed to be. But after a couple of years, we realized that we weren't ready to let go of all the opportunities for good sex.

Giles was my priority in life and I was his. We had a great sex life together but we both knew that we wanted to be able to enjoy sex with other people. Giles thought it was fair for both of us because while he liked to play the submissive role sometimes and was into some rough play, I just wasn't comfortable with that, and this gave him the freedom to play with some dominant men. Plus, I was bisexual and I liked being with women sometimes. Giles was rarely attracted to women.

Club Sin was our favorite place to go. We usually went together and either found someone that wanted some group fun or went off into different rooms on our own. It depended on what opportunities came up. But the beauty of Club Sin was that we never had to see the same person or people more than once if we didn't want to.

We didn't really have rules about seeing someone more than once. Giles saw a Dom for a few months. Generally, though, it was just simpler. Club Sin had rules, and assuming that everyone stuck with them, we felt safe. We always used condoms with other people, just to be on the safe side, and we had regular STD check ups but we found that most people who went there came with their most recent STD test results on their phone.

Most of the people who had STD results on their phone just had them in PDF form and they weren't easy to read. That's where Giles came up with his idea. An app so that swingers, ethically non-monogamous people, and others like us could share results safely and privately. The results would be easy to read. They couldn't be screen-captured. And they could be shared with a QR code. Like I said, Giles was a genius. It sounded simple but the amount of work that went into the security end of things was massive.

The club wasn't too busy when I got there. I found a table and ordered a drink and a bite to eat. I was early. I liked being early, though. It gave me a chance to see everyone come in and observe.

As I ate, I watched more people come in the door. As per usual, there was a real mix. Lots of couples, mostly hetero; but a lot of singles, too. The singles were often gay or bi. The women always came in with a partner or with girlfriends. Most women weren't single, though. And that was fine with me.

I was very careful with women because I didn't want anyone getting hurt. A lot of women said they were fine with one-time situations but many of them wanted more. I know that women are capable of no strings attached fun but I would rather be careful than hurt anyone.

After a couple of hours, the dance floor was full. I talked to a few people who knew me. Some were previous encounters. Others were just friends in the lifestyle.

Then she walked in. Well, *they* walked in. She was stunning on her own but there was something about the two of them together and I couldn't stop looking at them. There was a sense of confidence and togetherness. It wasn't that they were overly touchy or that he was possessive. I don't know. Whatever it was, it drew me to them.

I watched them go to sit at the bar and order drinks. The music was loud so they leaned in close to talk to each other. I was sure I'd never seen them here before. They looked a little nervous. Maybe just there to watch and get a feel for the place?

No, he was definitely cruising the room with his eyes. She was, too, but she was more subtle. And so stunning. Her long, dark hair flowed over her shoulders, and her tanned skin was a perfect contrast to the curve-hugging white dress she wore. Her make-up was minimal but she didn't need it. She looked like she had just stepped off a beach in Greece or something.

He was hot, too. Not especially my type but still hot. His blue shirt fit him perfectly, stretching over a broad chest and thick biceps. It was open just enough that I could see that he was equally tanned.

I didn't realize I was staring until her eyes met mine. He was saying something in her ear at the time, so he didn't notice her noticing me. I almost blushed. But she held my gaze with confidence and gave me a little smile. That was all I needed.

I got up and approached them. He saw me come over and stood up. I thought for a minute that he was going to tell me to fuck off and quit looking at his wife but then he smiled and I knew I was welcome. Wanted even? Was he looking me up and down?

"Hi," I said. "I'm Hunter. I've never seen you two here before. Is this your first time?"

He nodded and reached out his hand, "It is. I'm Kieran. This is Neve."

"What do you think of the place?" I asked.

"It's not what we expected," Neve said. "It's so classy. I half expected orgies on the dance floor."

"That's only on Saturdays," I said. Then I saw her raise an eyebrow and I laughed. "Kidding. No orgies on the main floor. It's for eating, drinking, dancing, and socializing only."

They laughed with me.

"Well, it seems great," Kieran said. "I assume there's more to the club than what we see here?"

I nodded. "Yes. There are private rooms upstairs. Thirty of them. Each room has a specific purpose, although it isn't absolutely necessary to stick to the purpose. The use of the room can be fluid."

Neve looked thoughtful and then she asked, "What kind of purpose? Like, themes?"

"Yes, I guess you could say that," I replied. "For example, there's a voyeur and exhibitionist room. Usually, there's a couple that likes being watched and people who like watching. That door is always open and there's a lot of people that like to be watched so it's always busy. There's a room where a Dom/me and subs can get flogged or spanked or whatever their thing is. There's a room for almost everything."

"Interesting," Kieran said. "What's your favorite room?"

"Me? I'm all about the pleasure of giving so I like to find a couple that wants to come to Room Twenty-Five with me. The multiple pleasure room."

"What does that mean?" Neve asked.

"It depends on who I go in there with. Sometimes it's two men and then I'm all about servicing them in whatever way they choose. I'm dominant but I'm more of a pleasure Dom, I guess you could say. I'm not into the pain," I explained.

"So, you're gay?" Kieran asked.

"No, bi. I love women, too," I said, giving Neve an appreciative look. "If I go into the room with a couple I might be of service to both of them. Or both of us might be focused on her."

I could see Neve squirming in her chair. Kieran had a smirk on his face.

They may have come here with the intention of just watching and observing but Neve was curious and Kieran was totally interested. He hadn't said it explicitly, but his body language communicated that he was into me as much as he was into her.

"I'm going to take a little walk. Boys room," I said. "I'd be really happy if you two were still here when I got back. But if not, it was great meeting you."

I turned and walked away. I knew their eyes were on me. I wanted to give them the opportunity to talk. If there was any doubt in either of their minds, I didn't want them to feel pressured. I was hoping they had figured out that I was interested in joining them in a room and would realize that I was giving them time to discuss it.

I often found men that wanted to watch me fuck their girlfriends or wives. And I was good with that. I could be the bull. Some of them wanted to be cucked. Others just liked to watch. But it wasn't often that I found a couple where the man was bisexual and wanted to be part of it and I was hoping my instincts about Kieran were right.

Mostly, I was hoping to have a chance to hear Neve moan as she got to experience multiple pleasures.

I washed my hands slowly at the sink and returned when I thought they'd had enough time. They were still at the bar, watching for me to return.

"You're still here," I said. "Would you like another drink?"

Neve shook her head.

"Would you like to come upstairs with me and see if Room Twenty-Five is open?" I asked.

Kieran's eyes lit up and Neve nodded.

"Can we talk about it first? Before we do anything?" she asked.

"Of course, Neve. This is all about you." I turned and looked at Kieran and said, "And you, too, if you like."

They stood up and I said, "One minute." Then I turned to the bartender and asked for three bottles of water. He passed them to me over the counter.

"Hydration," I said, passing them each a bottle. "You might need it."

Chapter Three: Neve

I was nervous but I tried not to show it as we followed Hunter up the stairs. It was ridiculous. It wasn't like I hadn't had a threesome before. But this was different. Each previous threesome was with partners I was familiar with and cared about and I knew cared about me.

There was something about Hunter I was drawn to, even before he got up and walked across the room. Confidence? Maybe. But lots of men were confident.

When we started talking, he was so respectful. He didn't hit on me and he wasn't pushy. I liked the way he gave us time to talk before inviting us upstairs. Hunter's whole attitude was attractive.

And of course, it didn't hurt that he was sexy as fuck! His broad shoulders were several inches above my head and the chiseled jawline made him appear ultra-masculine. Yet he said he was all about the pleasure. I couldn't have denied that I was very curious and very turned on.

When we got upstairs, he took us down a hallway with lots of rooms. Many of them were open with people inside.

At the beginning of the hallway, Hunter looked over his shoulder and said, "If the door is open it's fine to look. If the ribbon is across the doorway it means the room is closed to others but if there's no ribbon it means others can come in and join.

I loved that the rules were so clear.

Finally, at the end of the hall, we came to Room Twenty-Five. The door was open, no ribbon, and no one was inside. Hunter stepped aside and let us go in.

"Door closed or ribbon on?" he asked, looking at me.

"Closed. Please."

He closed the door behind us. There was a big bed that stretched across one end of the room. Bigger than a king-size bed even. On the other end of the room, two loveseats were facing each other with a table in the middle.

I was glad I didn't have to sit on the bed right away.

"So, do you have any questions? Or any boundaries you'd like me to respect?" Hunter asked.

We looked at each other. "I don't know," I said. "We've never really had to negotiate this kind of thing before because the other threesomes we've had were with people that knew us well."

"Ok. How about if I ask questions and you can let me know?" Hunter asked.

Fifteen minutes later, all the questions were asked and answered. Hunter stood and took my hand, and then Kieran's and he guided us to the bed. As we stood at the edge, he turned and kissed me. A slow, easy kiss that gave me time to change my mind. Totally non-threatening.

Then, he turned and kissed Kieran. A firmer kiss. The kind I knew Kieran was a sucker for.

Kieran moved behind me and Hunter kissed me again. Kieran's hands moved up and down my body before he slipped the strap of my dress over my shoulder, then the other strap. Slowly, he peeled off my dress, revealing that I was wearing nothing underneath.

Hunter took a minute to step back and gaze upon my body. His eyes were filled with desire as he watched me move onto the bed. I watched as both Kieran and Hunter removed their clothing. I was used to Kieran's body so my eyes were mostly on Hunter and I wasn't disappointed. Tribal tattoos decorated his upper torso, making his muscles look even bigger. As Kieran turned and slipped out of his pants, Hunter scratched his nails over Kieran's back, over his ass, and then cupped his balls.

When both of them were on the bed beside me, I forgot everything. I just listened to the gentle hum of pleasure as it started to build in my head and closed my eyes to get lost in the feeling of two sets of hands exploring my body.

"Neve, tell me what you want," Hunter said. "Would you like me to watch first?"

I shook my head. "No. I want your tongue."

Kieran laughed. "She can never get enough of that."

With a smirk, Hunter said, "Well, let's see if we can figure out what is enough."

Hunter moved between my legs and pushed them apart slowly. I could feel him looking at me for a moment before his tongue made me jump in excitement. Then he started doing things that made me forget to breathe.

Kieran was good at oral but he had his tricks. Hunter was different but also extremely talented.

As Hunter devoured me, Kieran gave me all the breast attention I craved. I didn't usually have the chance to have both kinds of pleasure at once and it wasn't long before I was moaning and squirming under their mouths. When I felt two fingers slide inside me, I wasn't sure if it was Kieran or Hunter. It didn't matter. I was getting so close to coming.

The fingers inside me moved faster and I moved against them. And then I was screaming, "Yes, yes. Oh, shit, don't stop!"

My body quivered as I came hard.

But they didn't stop. Kieran moved between my legs and then it was his familiar mouth doing all the things he knew I loved. Hunter moved up beside me on the bed and kissed me. His hands fondled my breasts, rubbing the hardened nipples but he just kept kissing me. He wasn't in a rush and his kisses were so seductive.

Kieran could make this last if he wanted to but I could see that the theme of the room tonight was going to be "make Neve come until she taps out." It was only a few minutes before I lurched into another orgasm.

They took turns going down on me, playing with my breasts, kissing me, fingering me until I thought I really might pass out.

Kieran looked up from between my legs with a smile. "Had enough?"

When I could catch my breath, I said, "Maybe not enough. But let's move on to something different?"

I looked at Hunter. He was smiling like a fool and stroking his cock. It was the first time I'd had a chance to look and see how hard he was. I knew immediately I wanted that thick monster inside of me.

"Condoms are on the table over there," he said, nodding to the bedside table. "Would you mind grabbing one?"

I smiled. I liked that he didn't even suggest that he shouldn't use one. I rolled and grabbed one and straddled him to put it on. I moved up his body a little until I felt the tip of his cock against me and then slowly lowered myself over him. He was nice and thick and I gasped as I impaled myself, letting him fill me completely.

Opening my eyes, I saw Kieran watching me.

"You are so glorious, Neve."

As I moved up and down Hunter's thick shaft, his hands played with my breasts. Kieran watched from the side for a few minutes and when our eyes connected it just spurred me on. I shifted my focus to Hunter and let myself get lost in the moment. He was calm and relaxed. He didn't push or try to take control. He just let me do my thing and pace myself however I liked.

I was so immersed in Hunter's appreciation of my body, I didn't notice Kieran get up and move behind me. When he kissed my neck, every inch of my flesh ignited. He worked his way down my back until he was at the base of my spine. He kissed his way back up again and then pressed his body against mine. Hot. So hot.

Kieran's hand slid down my back until it was at the crack of my ass. He moved his hand lower and rubbed at my tight hole just a little. Not penetrating. Just massaging it. His hand moved lower and Hunter moaned. His eyes closed and I knew what Kieran was doing. He was caressing Hunter's balls as I gyrated over his cock.

I raised my body so that I could just keep his cock inside me and Hunter's eyes popped open, a big smile spreading across his face.

"Oh, my God, that feels good Kieran," Hunter said in a husky voice.

I knew where Kieran was going with this. I leaned forward, keeping the head of Hunter's cock just inside me but giving Kieran room to play. Hunter pulled me in and kissed me. He moaned into my mouth and I knew what was coming next. Kieran's tongue was moving over Hunter's balls and the lower part of his shaft and then....oh, yes. That glorious tongue of his lapped up over my ass and circled my tight ring. I moaned back into Hunter.

Kieran moved up and down, from my asshole to Hunter's base and then to his balls and then back up again. Over and over until both of us were panting into each other's kisses.

I wanted Kieran inside me.

I raised my body off of Hunter's length and arched my back, opening myself up to Kieran. I felt his tongue there for a moment, then Hunter smiled.

"That's awesome, Kieran. Your mouth is so hot," Hunter said.

"I'll come back to that later," Kieran said, "but right now Neve's got an empty spot that needs to be filled."

Hunter laughed and said, "Well, we can't have that, can we?"

I gasped as Kieran's cock slid inside me. So familiar, yet every time he fucked me, it was like the first time. He had this little bend in his cock that just made the first penetration so delightful and always made me gasp.

"You are so incredibly sexy, Neve. I can't get enough of you. But watching you ride Hunter's cock - that's just extra," Kieran said.

I heard him but I couldn't exactly answer because he was fucking me hard and taking my breath away. His cock hit all the right spots and I knew I was going to come again pretty soon. I might have held off a little longer except Hunter's hand moved between my thighs and found my clit. He rubbed at a pace that matched Kieran's thrusts with a firmness that was just what I needed.

"Oh, Jesus, you guys, fuck..." I moaned as my body contracted around Kieran's shaft. "Fuck, fuck..."

I tumbled over the edge and my mind flashed with all the colors of the rainbow. Hunter put just the right amount of pressure on my clit and suddenly I was gushing. Each time Kieran pulled almost all the way out and drove his full length inside me, I gushed more. I knew that Hunter was getting drenched and I couldn't even care.

Kieran came just as my body calmed down and I felt his release spill out inside me.

Hunter guided me to roll over and to the side of him. Before I could say anything, he was between my legs, licking up all of Kieran's come. Kieran lay beside me and Hunter leaned over and took Kieran's semi-hard cock into his mouth and cleaned him off.

"Oh, fuck. If you keep that up, I'm going to get hard again," Kieran moaned.

"Wouldn't that be horrible," I laughed.

Both of them laughed together.

"So, are you ready to tap out yet?" Hunter asked.

"Hell, no," I said. "I'm not nearly done. You're a little wet though. I hope you aren't bothered by that. I don't always squirt so I didn't think to warn you."

"Bothered? Definitely not. Aroused by it? Hell, yes. That's so sexy, Neve. When a woman comes like that it just means she's comfortable. That's always a good thing. So, is there anything in particular you'd like next?"

"I think it's more about you right now, Hunter. You have been doing a lot of pleasing so far. What would you like?"

"Well, there's a lot of things I like but let's keep it low-key this time. Why don't you roll on your side for me? Face Kieran," Hunter said.

I did and Kieran pulled me in close, my face snug against his chest. I loved inhaling his scent and this was something that I didn't normally get to experience while I was having sex.

Hunter moved behind me and I felt his cock tuck in between my cheeks. One hand wrapped around my body and found my breast. His thumb rubbed casually against my nipple, almost as if he didn't know what effect it would have on me. Kieran tipped my chin up so he could kiss me.

Then, so slowly, with Hunter's hand at my breast and Kieran's mouth on mine, Hunter slid inside me. Just the tip at first. He began to rock against me and more of his length slid into me. I didn't like that he had to use a condom but even with it, I could feel each glorious inch take me in a painstakingly slow precision. Once he was fully inside me, he held himself still for a moment.

"Hunter, fuck...I need more."

"Be patient, Neve. Be still. Enjoy," he said.

Kieran continued to kiss me like he was enjoying the ice cream that would never melt. His tongue dipped in and out of my mouth, and I couldn't focus on one pleasure. There was so much at once.

Hunter began to move again in short thrusts. Barely pulling in and out. I was constantly full of him but the sensations around my opening were intense. His hand moved from my breast, down my belly, and to my throbbing clit. I'd already come several times so it was really sensitive and when his fingers found it, my body jolted in pleasure.

Kieran's mouth moved from mine down my body, kissing my neck, my collar bone, my chest until he reached my breast. And then he buried his face in there and suckled.

"Hunter, more, please..."

He laughed lightly, "Okay, Neve. Whatever you want."

Hunter's pace increased and our three bodies moved together. He was still so controlled. He thrust deeply three times as he pulled out to the tip, then drove himself deep into my body. Again, he slowed it down. I could already feel an orgasm building again but he wasn't going to let me get there too fast. His fingers were barely touching my clit. Just circling the edges and occasionally flicking over the tip.

"Neve, you are so sensual. I can see why Kieran loves watching you with someone else. I could watch you in this state forever," Hunter said. "Unfortunately, I don't think I can keep this up much longer. Are you ready to come with me?"

"Yes. Oh, God, yes, please..." I moaned.

Hunter's other hand moved to my throat, snug but not tight, and he tipped my head up. "I want you to listen to Kieran. When he tells you to come, you come, alright?"

"Yes..."

Kieran moved up, replacing his mouth at my breasts with his hands. "My beautiful lady," he said.

I opened my eyes and looked into his. Hunter's fingers put more pressure on my clit and his pace increased. He thrust faster and faster inside of me, his hand on my throat, tightening just the slightest as he drove harder.

I closed my eyes. I was going to explode any minute.

"Open them, Neve," Kieran said. "Do you want to come?"

"Yessss...I can't..."

"Okay. Now, babe. Come for us," Kieran said, smiling into my eyes.

It was the most intense thing I'd ever experienced. Kieran looking into my eyes, Hunter thrusting behind me, his groan as his cock twitched and he came. And then I exploded. I screamed my pleasure as Hunter's hand tightened around my neck, just firmly enough to add to the whole experience.

My body was just starting to calm when I felt Hunter's mouth at my neck, biting down slightly. His fingers pressed down on my clit and he captured it between his thumb and index finger and pinched lightly, once, twice, three times. Suddenly my body was convulsing against his hand. Kieran's mouth lowered to mine and he kissed me passionately. My muscles tightened over Hunter's cock and as he pulled out, I squirted again.

It was at least five minutes before they released me and I lay there, eyes closed, smiling like an idiot.

"You're right," Hunter said. "She doesn't tap out, does she?"

"I told you," Kieran laughed.

"Well, I'd still like to see if I could get her to say she's had enough."

"I'd take that challenge," I said, with a big smile.

As we were getting dressed, Hunter said, "I normally don't see people more than once. But...I'd like to see you again."

"Both of us?" I asked.

"Well, yes. But, if you date separately, I'd like to call you, Neve. Maybe go out for dinner or something? Kieran?"

Kieran said, "Actually, we're polyamorous, and dating separately is our normal preference. We aren't actually swingers. This is kind of a first for us."

"So, if you're open to that," I said. "I'll give you my number."

"Okay," Hunter said. "I'll call you, for sure. But I will disclose that I am partnered, too. Giles is my long-term partner and we've never really been more than swingers. I need to talk to him about it and make sure that it's something we both agree on."

"Of course," I said. "I wouldn't expect anything less. We'd love to meet Giles sometime if he wants to meet us. Even if he doesn't want to be involved."

I gave my number to Hunter and he kissed me sweetly. "I will for sure talk to you again. And you, too, Kieran. At the very least, I'd love to play with you both again."

Chapter Four: Neve

After we got home that night, Kieran and I agreed that we'd both had a great time and Club Sin was definitely somewhere we wanted to go again. But my mind was full of Hunter.

Kieran said he liked him, too. He agreed that Hunter could potentially be a long-time partner for me if his partner, Giles, was okay with it. We wanted to meet Giles, though. In the past, we had learned that sometimes third-party communications could be misconstrued. So, even if Giles didn't want to be involved with either of us down the road, meeting once was our preference.

We would wait to see how things went. But honestly, Hunter had found his way inside my brain.

I tried to go about my business, working and doing the things Kieran and I did every day. Hunter was always there, though. Except when Kieran and I were making love. Our desire for each other only seemed to increase after the first night at Club Sin. We went to bed at night and played for hours. Or we jumped on each other in a frenzy and fucked like we hadn't seen each other in years.

It was on the third day after our night at Club Sin when I received a text from Hunter.

Hunter: *Hi, it's Hunter.*

Me: *Hi.*

(Should I put some emojis in there? Nah. He didn't seem like an emoji kind of guy. Instead, I added a GIF of a cute girl waving at him).

Hunter: *Sorry it took me so long to message you. Just life. But I've been thinking of you. Could we go to dinner this week?*

Me: *Yes, I'd love to. I'm free Thursday if that works for you.*

Hunter: *That works great. Can I call you tonight and make arrangements? I hate texting.*

Me: *Absolutely. I'll be waiting for your call.*

For the rest of the afternoon, I smiled like a fool. I got home and Kieran knew something was up, so I told him that Hunter was going to call and we were going to have dinner.

"Should I clear out Thursday night? In case you want to bring him back here?"

"No, I don't think so," I said. "I think I want to keep it to just a date on Thursday. I want to know how his talk with Giles went. And maybe what he had in mind for us. Would it be okay if I made plans with them to come here for dinner on Saturday so we can meet Giles and talk?"

"I think that would be a great idea," Kieran said. "I'll cook dinner for all of us."

Later that night Hunter called and we talked for an hour. The whole time, Kieran was sitting at the other end of the couch beaming at me. I knew he was happy to see me so happy. I wished that Kieran could find more love, though. It was harder for men to find someone interested in more than just hooking up but could deal with the fact that he was married.

Thursday night, Hunter and I met at Grundy's Steak House and Bar. I was happy with his choice of restaurant. I loved a good steak but I hated places where you had to dress up too much. I was a jeans and boots kind of girl and sometimes I felt like I didn't quite fit in at the fancier places. Kieran always said I stood out no matter what, but in a good way. I think he might be a bit biased, though.

When I walked in, I told the hostess the name our reservation was under, and she took me to the table where Hunter was waiting. He stood to greet me and hugged me. He smelled amazing - not aftershave scented. Just the smell of a freshly showered man and a nice soap. He was wearing a crisp white shirt, dress pants, and the shiniest shoes I'd ever seen.

"You look great, Neve," he said.

I felt underdressed in my jeans and knee-high riding boots. My shirt was a little dressier, and I'd chosen a deep red sleeveless blouse, which I left just slightly unbuttoned.

"Thanks," I said. "So do you."

"I hope you don't mind. I ordered a pitcher of beer and some cheese toast to start."

No sooner did he say that than the server came with the cheese toast.

"Perfect," I smiled.

"Would you like a few minutes?" the server asked.

"Yes, please," we both said. "Maybe more than a few," I added. "Give us about ten minutes to catch up."

She left and I turned back to Hunter.

"Is it just me that was nervous about tonight?" he asked.

Laughing a little, because I was nervous, I asked, "Why would you be nervous?"

"Well, I'll be honest. I haven't had a date - a real date that wasn't leading up to getting laid - in many years. Since I met Giles."

"How long ago was that?"

"About seven years," Hunter said. "Giles is...well, the only person I've ever loved that wasn't family."

"He's special to you."

"Very. We weren't swingers at first. But after a couple of years, we realized that we really liked sex and sometimes we just wanted...variety. So, we agreed on the swinging lifestyle. Our general rule between us was to only have sex with someone once. No entanglements. It has always worked for us. Ethical non-monogamy. Always consensual. But we always come home to each other," Hunter said.

"Why not just stick with that," I asked.

Just then the server came back. I'd have to wait for an answer.

We both ordered steaks with stuffed baked potatoes.

Hunter smiled. "I guess I need to answer that, hey?"

"Yes," I said. I knew that this was the toughest part but the more honest we were at the beginning, the better the chances that no one would get hurt. "I mean, no. You don't have to tell me anything you don't want to. But, I don't date people I don't feel are being completely open and honest with me."

"Is that what we're doing?" Hunter asked.

"I hope so. Is that what you want?"

He nodded. "Okay, why not just stick with what was working?. I guess we could. I could never see you or Kieran again. But there's something about you Neve - not the sex. Okay, well, partly the sex. But you have these vibes. You make me feel like I need to see more of you. Not just for the sex."

He laughed. "Sorry, I know I keep saying not just for the sex. But I guess for me that's new. I have thought about seeing other people again because the sex was just that good. Then I move on and forget about it. That's why I waited a few days before messaging you. I wanted to make sure that I wasn't just riding on a sex high. As the days passed, I couldn't get you off my mind. I wanted to know you."

"Well, that sounds like dating. Have you talked to Giles about that?"

"We have talked. A lot. He admitted that he's been with people that he wanted to see more of but because of our arrangement, he never pressed it. We talked about what it would mean for us. What if I fall in love with you? What if he falls in love with someone else? It's scary. I don't want to think about life without him." Hunter looked down at his uneaten cheese toast and then took a bite.

"You know what polyamory is?" I asked him.

"I do. I know a lot more about it now than I did in the past. I've been researching the hell out of it. Giles has, too. I didn't realize that it is a lot different than swinging."

"It is. It's harder in some ways. Because multiple relationships are going on. Not just fuck buddies. There's a lot of communication. Talking things out instead of holding back. If we were to start dating, you and me, I would expect you to talk to me. A lot. And if we are dating, it is you and me dating. Kieran can be friends with you, but you're not dating him and he won't get in the middle of you and me. Even if there's a disagreement between you and him. The same would be expected of Giles. I wouldn't accept him making decisions about our relationship," I told Hunter. "It can be challenging. But I promise you, if you put the time and effort into it, loving more than one can have such amazing rewards."

"I really do like you, Neve. I want to try. And I'll listen if you tell me that we need to talk about something. And Giles...he's agreed that he wants this, too. We're both a little concerned about jealousy and time constraints but we're willing to learn," Hunter said.

He reached out and put his hand on mine.

"Okay. Let's agree that we're dating. We're not in a serious relationship...yet. Will Giles come and meet us?"

"Yes," Hunter said. "He very much wants to meet you. At the least."

"Okay. How does dinner at our place sound? Saturday night? Kieran has already said he would cook."

"I like that idea. It will be relaxing. Let me just see if that night works for Giles."

Hunter picked up his phone and almost immediately it vibrated. It's almost like Giles was sitting there waiting to hear from him. Hunter messaged back and then turned to me.

"Saturday night it is, then," he smiled.

Our food came and we ate and talked. Hunter told me about his work, how he and Giles met. We talked about bisexuality, fitting into the queer community when you're married, and more about polyamory and swinging. We even talked about kink.

Hunter was a great conversationalist and I enjoyed talking with him.

Of course, I'd seen him naked already, so thoughts of his beautiful body and that glorious cock crossed my mind several times. I am human. I tried to keep that to the back of my mind, but it wasn't easy when we were talking bout sex and kink. I kept imagining the fun we could have together.

I looked at my watch.

"Do you have to get going?" Hunter asked.

"I hate to say it, but I do. I have to get up early for work tomorrow. And Kieran is going to want to know how our date went," I laughed.

"Do you tell him everything?"

I shook my head. "No, not everything. If we are sharing very personal information that doesn't affect him, I know there's a line. I'll tell him how the date went and what we've agreed to and stuff like that. But if it's a personal conversation, if you share things with me that are private, I know where to draw the line. Likewise, I hope you would do the same."

"Absolutely," Hunter agreed.

"And I won't bring my relationship with Kieran into our relationship. Like, if Kieran and I had a fight, I might tell you I was sad or upset that we had a fight, but I wouldn't disrespect Kieran by going into details. Does that make sense?" I asked.

Hunter looked a little relieved to hear that. "Completely. To be honest, it was something I was a little worried about. I don't want to come between the two of you."

I smiled at him.

He put some bills in the folder and pushed them to the edge of the table.

"What do I owe you?" I asked.

"Nothing, Neve," he said with a smile. "You never owe me anything."

I was definitely liking Hunter more and more.

He walked me out to my car. "I know that this was just a date to get to know each other better and talk and it's not supposed to lead to sex. But...I really want to kiss you."

"I'd be disappointed if you didn't," I said, moving closer to him.

He pulled me in with a smile, put his finger under my chin, and tipped my head up. Our kiss started gently but progressed quickly into a hair tugging, body-mashing kind of kiss that made me light-headed. It was a good thing he was holding on tight because I felt like my knees might buckle.

"Good night, Neve. I'm looking forward to seeing you on Saturday," he said.

"Me, too."

As he walked away, I quickly got in the car and sat down so I could catch my breath. Hunter was fucking hot and he already knew how to get my motor running. If he turned out to be as honest as he seemed tonight, I had a lot of hope for us.

Chapter Five: Kieran

I was so happy that Neve's date with Hunter had turned out well. I liked him and I knew that Neve really liked him. I didn't want to see her get hurt, but I knew it was her call as to whether or not her relationship with Hunter would proceed. A lot of her decision depended on our dinner with him and Giles.

I'd been cooking in the kitchen for hours.

"Are you sure you don't want help with something?" Neve asked, coming into the kitchen for the third time. This time, she was dressed, make-up on, and looking extremely beautiful.

"There is one thing..." I said, putting down the ladle in my hand and slipping out of the moderately stained apron I wore. I walked to the other side of the island and pulled her close.

She laughed. "Oh? And what's that?"

I kissed her. "That's all. You can go back to your wine now."

She sat on the other side of the counter. "How about if I just sit here and keep you company?. They won't be here for another half an hour and the dining room is all set up. There's a fire going in the living room for later."

"You look excited," I observed, turning to put the hors d'oeuvres in the oven.

"I am. I'm excited for me. But I'm kind of nervous about meeting Giles. What if he doesn't like us and decides that he doesn't want Hunter to get involved with me? Or us? Or anyone? I mean, this is something new to them," Neve said.

Stirring the sauce, I said, "I know. It's a risk. But Hunter did tell you that he and Giles did a lot of talking. I'm sure in the past forty-eight hours they've talked even more. Giles must be fairly open-minded about the whole situation, otherwise, they would have called and said they weren't coming, right?"

"I guess so," she said.

"Don't get too far ahead of yourself, Neve. That's what tonight is for. To meet them, give them time to ask questions. I'm sure once Giles learns that you won't get in the way of his relationship with Hunter, he'll be okay with everything."

"I hope so. I'm trying not to get too invested. But I like Hunter. He's the first man I've met in a long time that I felt any kind of connection with, you know?" she asked.

"Yes, I get it. It's not easy. It would be nice if we would have met someone that was already poly but you know as well as I do that just because someone says they're poly, it doesn't mean they might not turn out to be unsuitable or even toxic. It happens whether your monogamous or polyamorous."

She nodded. "Okay. Just breathe. If it is meant to be, it will be. We'll just be ourselves."

"That's right."

Just then the doorbell rang and Neve jumped. "Do you want to get that and take them to the living room for now? I just need to turn things down and I'll be right there."

As Neve left, I took a deep breath. The truth was, I needed a minute to get myself together. I was nervous and excited for Neve, but I was a little jealous. Not so much because Neve might be starting this new relationship I might not be part of but because I craved someone in my life that filled some of the needs I had.

Part of it was physical. I missed being loved by another man. Neve and I played with pegging, but it wasn't the same. And I missed having someone that liked some of the things that Neve and I didn't share. Neve was not an outdoorsy person and I didn't expect her to like all of the things I liked. I would have enjoyed having someone special in my life that loved hiking, fishing, and camping the way I did.

I turned all the knobs down low. Everything was done cooking. I just needed to get it ready to take to the table. I washed my hands and dried them and took a deep breath. What made Neve happy made me happy, I reminded myself; someday, she would feel the same happiness for me.

Hunter and Giles were sitting on the couch, close but not so close anyone would be uncomfortable. Neve was sitting on the loveseat opposite them. They both stood as I entered the room.

"Kieran. That food smells delicious," Hunter said.

"It's almost ready," I replied.

"This is Giles," Hunter said.

Giles moved forward with his hand out to shake mine. Before Hunter even introduced him, my eyes were on him. He wasn't tall but he was well built and he obviously took care of his body. He wore thick-rimmed glasses that made him seem intelligent. Giles was dressed casually in a black metal band t-shirt and jeans that showed off his slim hips.

"Hi," Giles said. "Hunter had told me so much about you."

Our hands touched and...did I feel something? Was there a look in Giles' eyes?

"All good, I hope," I said with a nervous laugh. Jesus. I sounded like an idiot.

"Very. You've got a great house," he said.

"Thanks. Would you two like a tour?" Neve asked.

"If there's time, I'd love that," Giles said.

Hunter laughed. "This guy loves house tours. You'd think it would be me that needed to see the house since I'm the architect but he can't get enough of looking at people's houses."

Neve took the lead and guided us through the house. As she talked, I watched Giles. He was listening to her, but I felt like he had one eye on me the whole time, too.

In the basement, she stopped at the entrance of the last room. "And this is...our special guest room."

"Why is it special?" Giles asked.

"Because we don't use it for family, usually, unless we need to. It's for when one of us has a guest. Possibly an overnight guest. One of our partners."

"Ohhhh," Hunter said. "So, if you want to spend time with a partner here? Do you spend the whole time here?"

"No," I said. "Just intimate times. We prefer to be friends with each other's partners, at the least. We want them to feel comfortable here. In the past, we've had dinners with partners or just hanging out. But we don't want either of us to feel the need to always have dates outside of the house. You'd both be welcome here any time. And if there was sex involved...well, this is your room. If you want privacy together, close the door. If you're open to having someone else join you, leave the door open."

Giles looked at Hunter and kind of giggled. "So, if I came over with Hunter and Hunter and Neve wanted to have sex, they could come down here. And if you or I or both of us wanted to join in and the door was open...we could."

I smiled at him. "Absolutely."

Neve and Hunter looked at each other and smiled. This was going very well so far and we all seemed pretty excited about it.

"I think it's time to eat," I said. "I'm going to get the hors d'oeuvres on the table. Neve, do you want to get the wine poured? Or whatever you'd like to drink."

She nodded and I went to the kitchen. I couldn't help smiling. Not only did Neve and Hunter look like they wanted to get in that room right then, but Giles...I was not expecting him.

When I brought the appetizers to the dining room, they were all looking pretty comfortable. I was beginning to think that Club Sin may have been the best thing to happen to us in a long time.

Hunter and Neve were saying goodnight in the entryway and I offered to walk Giles to the car.

"So, how are you feeling about all of this?" I asked him.

He leaned against the car and said, "You know, I have never been jealous about Hunter having sex with anyone. I know he is bisexual and he loves women. Even if he decides he wants to fuck another guy - no problem. But when he told me that he liked Neve and wanted to see her again, I was a little thrown off. Even after I read about polyamory, I wasn't sure if it could work for us. I was sitting by the phone the entire night when they went on their date. I was terrified that he was going to come home and tell me he was leaving me for her."

"Neve would never have allowed that," I said.

"I can see that now. Seeing the two of you together, and hearing about how you make your relationship work while having other relationships; not imposing rules on each other's relationships; all of that makes me feel a lot more comfortable," Giles said. "And meeting you."

"What? I don't have anything to do with how they run their relationship," I said.

"No, it's not that."

"I don't get it..." I said.

Giles stopped me and put his hand behind my neck and pulled me down to him. His lips met mine and my heart lit up. I was right. There was something between us. It wasn't just me.

"Now do you get it?" he asked.

I smiled. "I'll be honest, Giles. I felt it, too. But I don't know if I can have sex with you and then walk away."

"You misunderstand me. I know. Swingers. I want what you guys have. Sex is great but...I'd love to have something deeper. I love Hunter and I didn't expect to love seeing him giving Neve those flirty eyes. When I felt those first twinges of...whatever they are...when I met you, I thought, this is just me wanting to get laid. But as the night went on, I knew it was more than that. Do you want that? More?" he asked.

"I do. Can we go slow, though? I'm just worried about the four of us getting tangled up and things getting complicated," I said.

"What does slow mean for you?" Giles asked.

"A date?"

"Okay. We'll go on a date. Call me later and we'll set something up. No expectations." Giles handed me his business card.

Chapter Six: Giles

The drive home was quiet. I guess we were both lost in our own thoughts. I kept looking at Hunter and I could see how excited and happy he was. But when we got out of the car, he ran around to open my door and pulled me out and then he kissed me.

"What was that for?" I asked with a laugh.

"For being amazing. I love you more than ever now because you're willing to give me the chance to...love someone else. I love you for being who you are."

"I love you, too. In fact, I really need to show you. I've had a raging boner all night long," I said. It was true. Sure, Keiran got it started but Hunter kept it going.

"Well, I'm not going to complain about that!" he said. "Shall we get started in the shower?"

He took my hand and led me up the stairs to our room. I stripped off as I heard him start the shower.

Later, we lay in bed cuddling. I loved the way he was so comfortable with being tangled together like we were one person. Not just after sex. Every night. But it was always better after I came inside him.

"So," Hunter said, "Maybe I'm just being hopeful here, but...was there something between you and Kieran?"

I laughed. "Maybe...."

"And what did you think of Neve?" he asked.

"I liked her. A lot. I can see what you see in her. There's something so genuine and open about her you can't help but be attracted to her."

"Right? I couldn't pin it down at first. Why I liked her differently than other couples I've played with at the club. But that's it. She's just genuine. She doesn't pretend to be anyone but who she is. And she's accepting. If I had said that was it and just said goodbye to them, neither of them would have blinked an eye. They knew what we were all at the club for."

"Exactly," I agreed. "And even when I asked stupid questions, they didn't appear to be phased by them at all. They just gave me clear and concise answers. Kieran is...well, I liked him a lot. But Neve is awesome. I don't feel it often but...I could see having a foursome with them."

Hunter perked up. "Really? I would love that. You're usually not sexually attracted to women."

"I know. I don't even know if you would call it a sexual attraction. I'm not sure I'd want to have sex with her but I could enjoy her touch, touching her. She's just so sweet," I said. I didn't know how to explain it because Hunter was right. I was gay. Mostly. But I'd had intimate encounters with women before. Maybe homoflexible was the right way to describe it.

"Well, we don't have to think about that right now. But you're okay with me and Neve moving forward? Dating?" Hunter asked.

With a laugh, I said, "I'd better be. Because I have a date with Kieran this week."

"What? How come you didn't tell me until now?" Hunter asked with a grin.

"Well, my mouth was full..."

"I'm excited for you," he said. "Maybe Neve and Kieran were just meant to come into our lives."

"Could be," I said. "Now, if you could chill your bill, I'd like to fall asleep in your arms. Would that be okay?"

Hunter kissed the top of my head and said, "Always."

I woke up the next morning to a message from Kieran. He said he couldn't stop thinking about me and could we have dinner that night?

I quickly texted back that I'd love to and we made plans on where to meet. It was just dinner, I told myself. Nothing to get worked up about.

But I was worked up. All day long, I found myself staring at the computer screen and seeing numbers instead of code. How was I ever going to get this app rolling out on time? I had the money now, thanks to the funder, and he was anxious to get things going.

I managed to get through the day. Okay, I called off early and went home to shower. I wasn't getting a lot done, anyway. Hunter wasn't home yet. He texted me from the office and said he'd be working late and wished me a good night. He signed off by saying, "Take condoms!"

He knew I wasn't planning on sex that night. But he always insisted it was better to be safe than sorry.

I met Kieran at a trendy restaurant I'd never been to.

"What kind of food is this?" I asked him when I joined him at the table.

"Honestly, it's some kind of mix-up of ethnicities. I don't know. I just heard it was good. I hate eating out. I'd rather be hiking or fishing for my food," he said.

Laughing, I said, "Well, why didn't you invite me to go fishing, then?"

Kieran had a slight smile. "Ya, you'd likely have turned me down."

"No, I wouldn't have. I mean, maybe in the middle of the week I'd have said no. But if it was a weekend I would have taken you to my super-secret fishing spot. You'd have to pack an overnight bag and sleep in the same tent as me, though, and I'm sure that would be awkward," I said.

Kieran shook his head. "I would love that. I love camping, fishing, hiking, boating - anything you can do outdoors. I didn't think you'd be the type to like that kind of thing."

The server came and we ordered. I don't even know what I asked for. I just wanted her to go away so I could have Kieran to myself again.

"I know. Most people don't think I'd be into that stuff. But my dad took me and my brothers out camping all the time. We loved it. I'm good at computer stuff. I can code and create some cool stuff and sometimes, I get lost in what I'm doing for days. I forget to eat and Hunter has to drag me out of the office. But once I'm away from the computer, I have to do other stuff. To clear my head. And being outdoors is my favorite thing to do when I'm not working," I told him.

"What about Hunter? Does he like that stuff?" Kieran asked.

"He doesn't mind it. But if you gave him a choice between chopping wood or playing racquetball, he'd choose the latter. He likes to exercise but he'd rather do it indoors where it's warm. I took him winter camping once and we had to go home early because all he could do was complain about the cold," I laughed.

Through our dinner, Kieran and I talked like we'd known each other all of our lives. We talked about sex and desire and love and then we talked more about our favorite outdoor sports. As we talked, our knees bumped under the table. Our hands touched when we reached for the wine bottle at the same time. And each time, my heart jumped in my chest so hard I thought it would explode.

As we were walking to our cars, Kieran said, "Do you want to come back to the house with me?"

"For?" I asked.

"Whatever you like. More conversation. Or something else. I'm just not ready for this to end," he said.

"Is Neve there?"

Nodding, he said, "She is, but she's likely in bed. I'd just pop in and let her know I was back and you were with me."

"She'd be fine with that?" I asked.

"She would. I'm pretty sure she'd be thrilled. She knows I like you. But we don't have to have sex. We can. Just know that if we do, I'm not going to think of it as just sex. I like you, Giles."

He took my hand and leaned in and kissed me. Then he pulled me forward so I could feel every muscle in his body and kissed me harder.

I sighed. "Okay. I'm yours. Let's go."

Kieran told me to have a seat in the downstairs rec room. "What do you want to drink?" he asked.

"Just water," I said. "I do need to go home tonight."

"Only if you want," he said with a smile.

He came back a few minutes later with a bottle of water for both of us. He sat beside me and rested his hand on my leg and I swear to God, I got hard instantly.

Talking didn't last long. We were kissing on the couch like a pair of teenagers within a few minutes.

"Do you want to go to the bedroom?" he asked.

"I do."

"You're sure? I'm going to catch feelings fast if we have sex," he joked. I knew he was serious, though.

"I think it's too late for both of us," I said. I stood and took his hand and we went down the hall to their special guest room.

We were both naked in a matter of minutes and in a pile on the bed. Kieran kissed me as he reached for my cock. I know it's not the biggest cock in the world but Kieran didn't give any indication that he was disappointed. His hand slid up and down my shaft like it was the best cock he'd ever held.

He moved between my legs and I felt his warm breath on my thighs. Then, he completely enveloped my member with his mouth.

"Oh, good Lord, Kieran..." I moaned.

"Shush," he said. "Just enjoy."

"But what about you?" I asked.

He ignored me and started doing all sorts of amazing things with his tongue. I was doing everything I could think of not to come in his mouth.

Kieran enjoyed what he was doing but he knew how to keep me at the edge. He didn't let me come. He just kept going like it was the wildest party he'd ever been to.

ROOM TWENTY-FIVE: A MULTIPLE PLEASURE REVERSE

Finally, he rose up between my legs pushing them forward. His cock tapped against my thigh and I knew what he wanted. I nodded.

He leaned over to the table beside the bed and came back with a condom and a small tube of lube. I watched as Kieran slid the condom over his cock and then snapped open the lube with one hand. His lubed up finger slid easily into my ass but it made me gasp anyway. As he finger fucked me, he drizzled more lube over his fingers, pushing another one deep inside me.

"Kieran, for Christ's sake, I'm lubed. Just fuck me already!"

He smiled down at me before he slid every glorious inch of his cock deep inside me.

Later, as we were getting dressed, Kieran said, "You'll tell Hunter?"

"Of course. Should I not?"

"No. You absolutely should. I don't want anything to mess up the good thing we have going here. You and me. Hunter and Neve. Maybe some other combination of all of us?"

"Good," I said, kissing him at the door. "We seem to be all thinking the same thing."

"Listen," Kieran said, "I like you. I like Hunter. I don't want anyone to get hurt. So, if there's anything you or Hunter aren't sure about, just talk to us okay?"

"Okay," I said.

I texted Hunter from the car and then drove home.

Chapter Seven: Hunter

The past weeks have been great. I saw Neve and we started having sex, just the two of us. Giles and Kieran were seeing each other regularly and had even gone on a weekend camping trip. Giles invited me to come with them but he knew I would say no. Camping had never been my thing. Plus, the nights were getting pretty cold.

Plus, it allowed me to spend the weekend with Neve.

It was more than amazing. It was perfect. I still loved Giles and I knew he was just as much in love with me as he ever was. But I think I was falling for Neve.

There was so much to talk about. Even for Neve and Kieran. As they said, every poly relationship is different and this was new to them because they'd never dated a couple. Our dates often turned into double dates, either at their house or ours. The four of us hanging out and eating and playing games just seemed like the most natural thing in the world.

I hadn't been with both Kieran and Neve since that night at the club but I thought about it sometimes. I talked to Giles about it and he was more and more interested in joining us.

One night, just before Kieran and Neve left our house, I said, "What do you guys think about heading to Club Sin this weekend?"

Neve asked, "All four of us?"

I could see her looking at Giles.

"Yes," he said.

"I thought...you were gay?"

He moved across the doorway and kissed her lightly.

"I'm flexible," he said. "At least I am now. I adore you, Neve. I love the way you make Hunter so happy. I can see what he sees in you. And I haven't been with a woman in a very long time but I have thought about it with you. And Kieran. And Hunter. Could there be a better way of bonding the four of us?'

She blushed.

"And all of you are okay with this?" she asked.

"If you are," I said.

"Okay. Let's meet at the club on Saturday. We'll see how it goes," she said.

Saturday night the club was packed and I hoped that we could get my favorite room. Room Twenty-Five could be in demand, at times. Even before we got drinks, I said to Giles, "I'm going to put the room on reserve. Just in case. If it turns out we don't need it, I'll let them keep the deposit and someone else can use it later."

"I'll get us a table and some drinks," he said. "Do you think Neve will change her mind?"

I shook my head. "I'm sure it will be fine."

I went to talk to the owner and set it up.

When I got back, Neve and Kieran were sitting with Giles. I sat between Neve and Kieran. I wanted to let Giles and Neve have a chance to talk.

At first, our conversation was light and relaxing. But I could see the chemistry between Giles and Neve building.

"Kieran, let's get some more drinks," I said.

As we got up, I leaned down to Giles and said in his ear, "Ask her to dance, dipshit."

That worked. As we stood at the bar, I saw the two of them get up and move to the dance floor. I knew Giles loved dancing. I was not much of a dancer. If I got drunk I'd get up there, but I was pretty sure I looked like a flailing cow.

Giles and Neve did not. They were perfect together. And they were so fucking sexy.

I turned to Kieran. "Did you know Neve could dance like that?"

He gave me a look. "Okay, of course you did. Look at them. Don't they look great dancing together?"

"They do," he said. "But it seems like there's a little more than dancing going on."

I looked back at the dance floor. He was right. It was pure foreplay. Their hands were all over each other. Not in a dirty kind of way. It was sensual and it was exciting to watch. It made my dick ache a little.

The bartender passed us the drinks and we went back to the table. We watched them move together like they were sliding around on satin sheets. Then, their bodies combined and they were making out.

I turned to Kieran. "Looks like our foursome is on. You're good with it?"

"Absolutely. I've always enjoyed threesomes with Neve and we had a great time with you. Now, four people that care about each other? I can't imagine how it could be any less than amazing."

When they finally came back they were hot and sweaty. Kieran's hand was on my cock under the table, stroking me through my jeans. I was eager to get upstairs.

I didn't want to rush them, so I let Kieran keep stroking as Neve leaned over to kiss me.

"I want you."

So much for not rushing.

She leaned over the table and kissed Kieran, "And I want you."

Then she moved in to kiss Giles, "And I want you."

Giles was grinning ear to ear.

"So, this is happening?" he asked, looking around at all of us.

Everyone nodded.

"Let's just take a step back and finish our drinks," Kieran suggested.

Neve looked disappointed but she sat down anyway. She reached for her drink and gulped it back in one go.

Putting it down, she said, "Drink up, boys."

Chapter Eight: Neve

I'd be the biggest liar if I tried to act casual. From the moment I got on the dance floor with Giles, all of my nerves were lit up. He was an amazing dancer and I could see that he was just as aroused by my dancing as I was by his.

I was still a little nervous. I'd never been with three men before. Two men were one thing but three? That was a lot of cocks. Could I manage it?

Then I reminded myself that Kieran and Giles were into each other and Hunter was into Giles and Kieran. But they were all into me.

I could see the look of amusement on their faces as I slammed my empty drink on the table. "Drink up, boys!"

They laughed. I knew that drink might hit me hard, so I said, "I'm going to go to the ladies' room and then get some bottled water. Y'all better be caught up by the time I get back."

I needed a minute to get my head together, anyway. And freshen up. Giles said he wasn't normally attracted to women and the fact that he saw something in me was a bit of a turn on. Plus, I really liked him. In the past few weeks, the four of us had spent a lot of time together. We all had something in common. It was like having three boyfriends. Sure, I hadn't had sex with Giles. Yet. But there was an intimacy between us that was not like anything I'd had with someone that was just a friend.

When he kissed me the other night, I couldn't have been more surprised. I honestly didn't realize that he was that flexible. Or that he thought of me that way. But his kiss was so incredibly sweet and vulnerable. I wanted to get naked with him right then and there.

I knew this was going to be something truly awesome. Hunter and Kieran and Giles and me in one bed. I didn't know how it would go but it had to be good, didn't it? Of course, it did. There was just so much love and chemistry between us.

I didn't know how Hunter felt about me yet. Sure, we'd been dating, having great sex, but he hadn't said anything more than that he liked me a lot. But I knew how I felt. I was head over heels in love with the man. There was love for Giles, too. And of course, for Kieran.

When I came back, their glasses were empty. They all stood up.

"Lead the way, Neve," Hunter said. I took Giles' hand and Kieran's and Hunter walked behind us as I led us all up to Room Twenty-Five. Our playroom for the night.

When we were all in the room, I closed the door. Hunter immediately took off his clothing and lay on one side of the bed. Kieran followed suit and lay on the other side of the bed. I was next to get naked and I snuggled my ass into Hunter. Jesus. The man was already hard. Giles was last to take his clothes off and he took the last space on the bed between me and Kieran.

I moved in closer to Giles.

"What does this look like for you, Giles? Is there anything you want?" I asked him.

"I want...to feel you. Your skin. Your hands. Your mouth. It's different from being with a guy. Just go slow, okay?"

I nodded. I knew that Giles was stepping out of his comfort zone so I kind of wanted to make sure he was especially comfortable.

My hands moved up and down his body and he closed his eyes and let me touch him. I didn't touch his cock, although it was already growing. Kieran was kissing his neck and grinding against him. I guessed he was likely hard, too.

Three hard cocks for me to play with.

I took my time with Giles. Moving in to kiss him, our bodies not touching yet, I felt him shiver. When he opened his eyes, he smiled at me.

"More?" I asked.

"More," he answered. "Actually, would you...?"

He hesitated.

"Tell me, Giles," I said in a husky voice. I wanted him to know that I was excited about pleasing him.

"Would you suck my cock? It's different from a man doing it, and..."

"No explanations necessary."

I moved between his legs, crouching over my knees, and held him in my hands. I wanted him to enjoy it so I took my time. I licked up and down his shaft and felt his body jerk.

"Mmmmm," he moaned.

Then, I took him in my mouth with just my lips. I locked them around the base of his shaft and moaned with him. My tongue flatted along the underside of his cock and I moaned again. I could feel his breath quicken.

Kieran and Hunter stayed off to the side, watching I guessed. I kept all my attention on Giles, for now.

I slowly moved my mouth, up and down the length of his cock. When I got to the top, I swirled my tongue around the head before plunging down to take him all again. I used every trick I had to make it last.

I got distracted when I felt one of them, I'm not sure who, move behind me. I felt a body between my legs and then warm breath against my thighs. Then a tongue dipping in and out of my opening. Whoever it was reached for my hips and pulled me down to his mouth. I moaned again and Giles moaned with me.

I wasn't expecting to feel the cool lube drizzle against my ass and I gasped as a finger slipped inside me. I knew it must have been Kieran because Hunter and I had never discussed anal play before this. Kieran knew I loved it.

This was a completely different combination of feelings than I'd ever experienced before. Kieran's fingers slid in and out of my ass as Hunter devoured me from below. I could barely concentrate on what I was doing to Giles anymore.

When Giles pushed me back a little, he said, "I'm not going to last much longer if you don't stop, Neve."

"That's okay," I smiled as I looked up at him.

"Not yet," Giles said.

Giles slid out from under me and Kieran replaced him. He kneeled in front of me and said, "You are so amazing, Neve."

His cock was hard and I wanted him in my mouth as much as he wanted my mouth on him.

I couldn't see where Giles went but I heard him moving at the end of the bed. "Legs up, Hunter."

And then I heard Hunter grunt as he continued to lick me. I could feel the movements and I knew Giles was fucking Hunter. Kieran had the best view. He could look down and see me sucking his cock or look behind me and see Hunter with his head between my thighs as Giles held his legs up and fucked him.

The number of combinations we came up with that night. I got fucked. Kieran got fucked. Cocks were sucked. When one of us needed a break, we just rolled over and watched for a bit.

The end of the night was amazing, though. The best thing I could have ever imagined.

There was something that Kieran knew that I wanted for a long time that neither Hunter nor Giles could possibly know.

I was riding Hunter, just like the first time we were together. Giles had cleaned up after fucking him and now, he was sliding his cock in and out of Hunter's mouth as I watched. It was so erotic. Seeing the two of them together made me fall for them even more.

Kieran was laying on the other side of us when he said, "Babe, you know that fantasy?"

"Which one?" I asked.

"You know. The one you've only told me."

I knew instantly.

"Yes," I said.

"Now?"

"Yes. I'm exhausted. I have just enough left in me for one more orgasm," I said.

He nodded. I heard him get up and move behind me, positioning himself between Hunter's legs.

"Hunter, pull her close,"

"What's going on?" Hunter asked. He looked at me with concern.

"It's okay. I want this. I want you and Kieran both inside me," I told him.

Giles stroked his cock and said, "That's so fucking hot."

A grin spread across Hunter's face. "I'm in."

I laughed. "That's kind of the point. I've never done this, so let's just take it easy, okay?"

He nodded.

Kieran was fingering my ass again.

"I can feel his fingers against my cock," Hunter said. "Damn, that's amazing."

Kieran pulled his fingers out and I could feel his cock pressing against me. He had his cock in my ass many times before. It was something we both enjoyed. But a double penetration wasn't as easy to pull off as it looked in porn.

Hunter slipped out.

Kieran slipped in.

We wiggled about for a few minutes before Hunter was able to squeeze his way back in.

And then just like that, they were both inside me and I felt more full than I'd ever felt in my life. They weren't even moving and my muscles were contracting around them both.

"Are you okay, Neve?" Giles asked.

"Shit. Fuck. Yes. Very okay." I could barely talk.

They began to move. So slowly, but I felt every inch of their flesh inside me. They figured out a rhythm where Kieran pulled out and

Hunter thrust in. Hunter pulled out and Kieran slid inside my ass again. Once they got that rhythm going, they moved faster and I couldn't hold back.

My body erupted into an orgasm that my body and mind were not prepared for. I felt it in my eyes, my teeth, and I'm sure there were some internal organs that were shuddering in intense release. As Hunter receded and Keiran pulled in, I squirted. There wasn't much room, though, so it escaped out the sides in a gush.

"Holy shit, are you okay, Neve? Oh my God, you're squirting. Oh my God..."

"Giles, shut up. I'm going to come," Hunter said. "Can you come now? In my mouth?"

Giles immediately turned to Hunter and put the tip of his cock in his mouth. He stroked and came as Hunter screamed out his release. Kieran lost it and drove his cock deep in my ass as Hunter slipped out of me. My mind was done but my body had one more in me and I convulsed under Kieran's deep thrusts and we both came.

It took a minute before we could move. Kieran hunched over me. Giles collapsed beside us. And Hunter lay there with a big grin on his face and a bit of Giles' come on his cheek. I leaned over and licked it off before I squirmed out from between Hunter and Kieran.

After a few seconds, Kieran came to lay on my other side. We were all sweaty and gross but we cuddled in together anyway.

After a bit, Hunter said, "Holy shit."

Giles laughed, and soon we were all laughing.

"I can't imagine doing that with anyone but you three," Giles said. "I love you guys."

I didn't know if he meant it "that way" or not, but I didn't care.

"I love you all, too," I said. "You are all so special to me."

"So, are we a fourple now?" Hunter asked.

"A what?" Kieran laughed.

"You know. Like a throuple. But four people," said Hunter.

ROOM TWENTY-FIVE: A MULTIPLE PLEASURE REVERSE
HAREM ROMANCE   61

"We are us. You and me," I said, kissing Hunter, "and you and me," I said, kissing Kieran. "And you and Giles and Kieran and Giles. And now me and Giles."

Giles suddenly got serious. "Does that mean no more swinging?"

Kieran shook his head. "Only if that's what you want. No one owns anyone. I don't own Neve. We are all free to love how we want to love - or fuck how we want to fuck. But Neve and I do have some boundaries. Not as a couple but as individuals. We'll have to talk some more, I guess. But can that wait? I can't even think straight."

Hunter laughed. "Me, too. I think whatever it is, we can work it out. Because we love each other and I think you all are worth working for. All I know is that I want you all in my life."

We all nodded. I think we dozed off for a second. Maybe more.

There was a knock on the door and we heard a voice.

"Hey. The club is closing. You don't have to go home. You just can't stay here."

My eyes blinked open and Hunter said, "Our place? We have the king-sized bed."

Epilogue: Four Years Later

Giles

"Kieran, would you please come and help me round up these two for bath time," I called. Kieran was getting the kayaks ready for our trip this weekend.

He laughed and put down the rag he was using to wipe them down. He scooped Honey up with one hand while I chased after Gillian. Only three years old and the damn kid was faster than me. She gave me a look that was pure Hunter but then when I tickled her I could swear her giggle sounded just like me.

When Neve found out she was pregnant, we discussed getting a paternity test to see who's baby she was having but we decided it didn't matter. We all loved her. We'd all had unprotected sex with her.

About a year after seeing each other, Hunter and I decided that we didn't want to have random sex anymore. We just weren't interested in it. So, we approached Neve and Kieran about becoming fluid bonded. There was still the possibility that one of us might want to have another partner (Kieran had started seeing this woman named Kaili) and we knew condoms were important outside our circle but after we were all tested for STDs and made the promise not to have unprotected sex with other people, we let the condoms slide. We were meticulous about getting tested every three months but it was worth it to know that we could keep each other safe.

A couple of months after that, Neve said she wanted a baby. She went off birth control and ten months later the twins were born. No one knew who the father was. We were all the fathers. Kieran was Pops, I was Daddy, and Hunter was Papa.

Neve called out, "Are those two still playing outside? Get them in here, you guys!"

Neve

I love watching the guys chase the girls around. I know Honey and Gillian are a challenge. They have so much energy and they are already getting sassy, but they have brought so much more love into our lives.

I rubbed my hand over my swollen belly. I was hoping for a boy this time around, but I'd be happy no matter what.

"Hunter has the bath ready for them," I said. "Take them right upstairs and then they can come down for dinner. It's almost ready."

They took the giggling pile of girliness upstairs, both Kieran and Giles laughing with them.

Giles came down a minute later and said, "Kieran and Hunter are taking care of bath time. Can I help you with supper?"

"Sure," I said.

More love meant more hands to help.

Hunter

Gillian laughed as she splashed water at Honey. Honey pouted.

"She's just playing baby," I said. Honey was the more sensitive of the two.

"Papa, tell us the story of when you built our house and when we all came to live here," Honey said. Her voice was as sweet as her name, and even though I'd told her the story a hundred times in the past month since we moved in, I couldn't refuse her.

"Well, we all needed a place to live, so I built us a house. We all moved here so we could be a loving, happy family."

Sometimes that was enough. Not tonight, though.

Gillian splashed and said, "No! The real story, Papa!"

Kieran laughed with her and said, "Ya, the real story!"

He could have told it just as easily, but the girls said I was the only one that told it right.

Kieran

We brought the girls downstairs smelling fresh and sweet in their pj's.

"Took you long enough," Neve said.

"They made me tell the story again," Hunter said, rolling his eyes.

"Please," she laughed. "You love telling that story, and you love that they only want you to tell it."

"Okay, it's true."

I looked around the big table we ate supper at every night and my heart swelled. So much love in this room. Hunter held Neve's hand as she lowered herself to her seat. She was almost due. Only a couple more weeks and there would be another child to add more love to our lives.

We all sat and ate. The girls bickered. Gillian refused to eat her peas until Giles gave her that look that only worked when it came from him. Then she pouted and shoveled them all in her mouth so she would get it over with.

Giles, Hunter, Neve, and me. We thought we were the only family we would ever need until Gillian and Honey came into our lives. We realized then, it wasn't about what you need. It was about accepting whatever love came into your life and cherishing the hell out of it.

I hope you enjoyed Room Twenty-Five of the Club Sin series! Check out Room Twenty-Six: Primal Cravings[1] by Vanessa Brooke for more Club Sin fun!

1.   https://www.amazon.com/gp/product/B09C2G1BRZ

Don't forget to rate! Indie authors like me depend on readers like you to rate and review their stories. It makes it easier for others to find them and lets other readers know what you think! Thanks!

Don't want to miss one of my new releases? The best way to keep up with what I've been publishing is to subscribe to email updates. You can do that here: http://eepurl.com/D6Lu9

Find me everywhere (Twitter, TikTok, Instagram, and more)! Check out new releases. Discover hot short stories to read for free. Everything you could desire is here: http://inkyblueallusions.com

Also by Autumn Seave

Club Sin
Room Twenty-Five: A Multiple Pleasure Reverse Harem Romance

Standalone
Sorority
Essays on Sex, Sexuality, and Polyamory
The Triangle
Between Friends

www.ingramcontent.com/pod-product-compliance
Ingram Content Group UK Ltd.
Pitfield, Milton Keynes, MK11 3LW, UK
UKHW020746110325
4940UKWH00041B/904

* 9 7 9 8 2 2 3 8 2 6 5 9 0 *